Holly

Book Two

Christmas on Dewberry Lane

Cheryl Wright

Holly

Christmas on Dewberry Lane
Book Two

Copyright ©2020 by Cheryl Wright

Cover Artist: Black Widow Books

Dedication

To Margaret Tanner, my very dear friend and fellow author, for her enduring encouragement and friendship.

To Alan, my husband of over forty-six years, who has been a relentless supporter of my writing and dreams for many years.

To Virginia McKevitt, cover artist and friend, who always creates the most amazing covers for my books.

To You, my wonderful readers, who encourage me to continue writing these stories. It is such a joy knowing so many of you enjoy reading my stories as much as I love writing them for you.

Table of Contents

Chapter One

Dewberry, Montana

November 1880,

"Quick, run! Get out now!"

Holly Yates' head shot up as the fireman ran into her store, the *Holly-Berry Cake Shoppe*. Confusion surrounded her. "Wha…" Before she had a chance to speak further, he'd come behind the counter and swooped her up. "Put me down this instance!" she demanded. But he did no such thing.

"You're in danger, Ma'am," he said as he quickly carried her out onto the street. It was then she noticed the horse-drawn steam-driven fire engine out on the street in front of her store.

"I said, put me down," she said through gritted teeth as she stared into his chocolate brown eyes, not taking her gaze from his. He continued to carry her in spite of her demands. "What on earth is going on?" Her last words were undecidedly a demand, and the burly man holding her slowly put her down. Holly knew if she'd been on the ground already, her hands would have been on her hips, without doubt. She was fuming at his indiscretion and his assumption he could man-handle her without permission.

He pointed upwards, toward the flames coming out of the roof of her store. Holly's heart pounded. This was the last thing she needed, and not long before Christmas too – her busiest time of the entire year.

"Darn it," she said. "I've been putting off replacing that old oven for ages. I guess I have no choice now."

He stared at her but uttered not a word.

"It is the oven, I presume," she asked, suddenly not so sure.

"We'll have to wait and see. If you're all right…"

She waved him inside. The *Holly-Berry Cake Shoppe* was her livelihood. Without it, she had no idea what she would do.

"What's going on? Are you all right, Holly?" It was Mrs. Grayson, a lovely lady, but the town gossip.

"I...I honestly don't know," she said quietly. "Apparently, my store is on fire." She'd not long put six Christmas cakes in the oven, and now they would be ruined. "This will destroy my business." No matter how much Holly wanted to put her hands to her face and cry, she was determined to be strong.

Mrs. Grayson reached out and rubbed a hand over Holly's back. "Don't jump to conclusions," the older woman said. "Wait until you know for sure." She looked up at Holly who was far taller. "You look pale, dear. Come and sit down." She led Holly to a wooden bench where they both sat quietly for a few minutes.

"That oven needed replacing months ago and I put it off." She swiped at an errant tear and the other woman scowled.

"Don't be so hard on yourself. It may not be the oven after all."

Holly nodded. Mrs. Grayson could be right.

Suddenly, the fire chief stood in front of the pair. "The fire is out but there's a lot of damage."

Holly bit her bottom lip. "Was it the oven?" Whether it was or not, Holly would have to replace it. The *Holly-Berry Cake Shoppe* only existed because of the inheritance from her grandparents, and she'd been thrilled, but there wasn't enough to start the store and buy everything she needed if she invested in a brand new oven, so she'd settled for a second-hand one. That seemed like a lifetime ago now, but it was a decision she had to make at the time.

She prayed she was wrong, but was almost certain she'd have to finally replace it.

"I'm sorry to have to tell you, Miss Yates, but the fire appears to have begun in the oven."

Holly sighed. Now there was no choice but to purchase a new oven. And this time, it would be new. She could have lost her entire business, and thanked the Lord it hadn't gotten that far.

Mrs. Grayson suddenly reached out and patted her hand. "Holly, dear," she said gently. "I will happily lend you the money for a new oven." It would be tight, but Holly thought she could manage it. She would prefer to not to have to borrow money to replace it. First, she needed to find out what she was up for. Her biggest worry was how long she would be out of business.

Somehow through the fog, Holly decided she could concentrate on slices and other items that didn't require an oven until the new one arrived. Yes, that was a good plan.

"Thank you, Mrs. Grayson," she said, feeling a bit more confident now. "Would you mind if I get back to you? It is a truly kind offer, and I'm incredibly grateful, I just need to check a few things."

"Of course, dear." They sat quietly on the bench together. Holly felt better now than she did just a short time ago, but did wonder whether her little store would even be open for Christmas this year.

Feeling deflated, Holly opened her store the next day, albeit far later than usual. She set to work making slices that didn't require the use of an oven. She'd already been to the mercantile to inquire about the cost of a new commercial oven, and after some consideration, put in an urgent order. The mercantile owner was mindful of her situation and promised to telegraph the order through immediately. It would likely still take at least two weeks.

In the meantime, Hank Spencer at the saloon offered for her to use his oven and kitchen provided it didn't interfere with his saloon's kitchen routine. Holly couldn't be more grateful.

Today she would make slices, and tomorrow she would start work in Hank's kitchen at dawn.

"Holly, dear," Mrs. Grayson said as she strolled into the store. "How are you coping?" What she really wanted to know, Holly was certain, was whether or not she needed to make a loan.

"I'm fine, thank you Mrs. Grayson. Although, I do admit to feeling a little out of sorts."

"Of course, my dear, of course," the older woman said, sympathy showing on her face. "I can't begin to imagine how you are feeling." She glanced about the store to ensure they were alone. "About that other matter. The one we discussed yesterday…" She glanced about again. "You will let me know if you need to take up the offer, won't you?"

Holly smiled tentatively. "I do appreciate your offer, Mrs. Grayson," she said quietly. "But after checking my accounts, I can manage. Thank you though." The last thing she wanted to do was go into debt to keep her business viable, but she still had time to make up for it with the Christmas rush. That was, provided the oven arrived in time. Installation was included in the cost she'd paid, which would shorten the process and would happen on the day of delivery. It helped ease her mind.

Patting her hand, Mrs. Grayson smiled. "Well, do let me know if you change your mind." She glanced about at the poor pickings available in the display cabinet. "You've done well to manage these," she said, pointing. "May I have four of those lemon slices? I know it's a bit naughty, but one has to indulge oneself now and then." She grinned then. Both women knew Mrs. Grayson indulged herself on a daily basis. But she was very kind-hearted and generous to a fault.

Holly bagged up the slices and handed them over. Mrs. Grayson dipped into her reticule and pulled out a wad of cash. "I'm certain I owe a tidy sum on my account by now," she said when Holly's jaw dropped.

"Not that much, surely." Holly opened her account book, and she was correct. "You only owe five dollars. There must be a hundred there," she said, handing most of the money back.

"Piffle," Mrs. Grayson said off-handedly. "Add it to my account as a credit. I'll use it up some time."

Was this the old dear's way of helping Holly out? She thought so, but didn't dare mention it. "Thank you. I truly appreciate it." She came around from behind the counter and gave the old lady a kiss on the cheek. Mrs. Grayson pulled her into a tight hug.

"Everything is better with a hug," she said as she released Holly from her embrace. "Was there much other damage?" she asked, craning her neck to try and see through to the kitchen.

"See for yourself." Holly opened the swing door that led through to the roomy kitchen.

Mrs. Grayson stopped in her tracks as she entered the kitchen. "Oh, my Lord!" she said. "You've done the right thing ordering a brand-new oven this time." She turned to Holly. "You did, didn't you?"

"I certainly did. I can't risk this happening again."

Mrs. Grayson walked over and studied the scorched woodwork. "You'll need a carpenter for this. Marcus Taylor can help you out. He doesn't charge an outrageous fee, either."

Holly screwed up her face in thought. "Do I know this carpenter? The name doesn't ring a bell."

Mrs. Grayson laughed. "Oh, you know him all right. He carried you out of the store during the fire." She looked rather pleased with herself, like the cat that stole the cream.

"That pesky fireman who refused to put me down?"

"The very same man," Mrs. Grayson said. "He's really quite nice when you get to know him."

Holly very much doubted it. He was a bully, and Holly didn't like bullies. "I doubt it," she said, pulling her face into a scowl again.

"Well, my dear, I don't know any other carpenters in Dewberry, so it's Mr. Taylor or no one."

Her heart thudded. "Well, I guess it's no one."

The surprise on Mrs. Grayson's face was priceless. "Now you're being stubborn. I'll have a quiet chat with Mr. Taylor and see what we can come up with." Without another word, she turned on her heel and left the store.

She was a generous old bird, but she'd gone a bit far this time.

Holly carried four dozen cupcakes from the saloon kitchen to her store. She would then return for the larger cakes she'd baked. It would likely take at least four trips to get her day's baking where it belonged.

For now, she had to settle with having a smaller supply than normal. Her customers would surely understand the catastrophic fire was going to make things difficult, but she was doing the best she could.

It was now three days after the fire, and she was settling into her new routine. It was tiring carrying everything across, but it had to be done. Hank Spencer from the saloon had found an old trolley in the basement she could use to cart everything to her store. It was rather rickety and not easy to push, but it still made things far easier.

She loved Dewberry and the people in it. When things got tough, everyone rallied around and helped each other out. Even those she barely knew had offered to help where they could. The community spirit was well and truly alive.

Pushing the unwieldy trolley into her kitchen, Holly glanced around. Practically everywhere she looked there was charred wood. The surrounds of the oven were the worst affected, but most of her cupboards and benches were scorched as well. Only not as badly. One end of her large wooden table, where she did most of her decorating, was damaged, but Holly thought it might be redeemable. At least she hoped so.

She placed the cupcakes on the clean table and turned to go back to the saloon. She saw the silhouette of a man standing in the store. It was still early, and the store had not even opened for the day yet. There wasn't a single item in the display case – didn't he realize there was nothing to buy at this hour of the day?

It wasn't that she didn't want customers; it was more that she had nothing to sell him. She straightened her back and wore a false smile. "Good morning," she said as brightly as she could manage. "As you can see, I have no baked goods as yet. Another hour or so and…" she spread her arms wide, trying to prove a point.

"I'm not interested in buying anything," he said, cutting her off. "I'm Marcus Taylor. Mrs. Grayson said you needed my help."

Didn't she tell the stubborn old lady she wasn't interested in Mr. Taylor's assistance? She was certain she did. "I don't need your help, Mr. Taylor.

I'm sorry Mrs. Grayson got you here under false pretenses." She began pushing the trolley toward the entrance to her little store.

"I'll just take a quick look, if you don't mind."

He didn't wait for an answer and made his way into the kitchen. She had been right all along; the man was a bully. "I do mind," she said, but he had already gone and didn't hear her protests. Holly abandoned the trolley and hurried after him. "Mr. Taylor," she said, exasperated. "I really don't…"

He turned to face her. "Now that all the smoke has cleared, I can see it is far worse than I originally thought."

Worse? Holly's heart thudded. The oven was costing a fortune, and now…what would it cost to replace her entire kitchen? "I…" What could she say? It had to be fixed if she were to resume her business, and that was certainly her plan. Holly felt the color drain out of her face. Of course, she had insurance, but it wouldn't cover anywhere near the costs she was facing. The insurance only covered the cost of the second-hand oven, so she'd lost out on that. It would depend on what Mr. Taylor charged whether her insurance would even touch the fees necessary.

"Are you all right, Miss Yates?" He stepped toward her. Did he think she would faint? She was made of stronger stuff than that.

"Perfectly fine, thank you, Mr. Taylor."

He stared at her for at least twenty seconds. "Call me Marcus, everyone does."

"Then you must call me Holly." She preferred the formalities with strangers, but since this person had carried her in his arms, they could perhaps drop formalities this time. "What is this going to cost me, Mr...er, Marcus?" She braced herself for the shock.

He smiled tentatively. "It's not as simple as that," he said, running a hand over one of the cupboards. "Some of this can be saved since it's only surface damage. Sandpaper will fix that, but here, around the oven," he pulled a chunk of charred wood from the surrounds to show her, "this is ruined. There is no choice but to replace it."

She swallowed hard. "And what will that set me back," she asked in a quiet voice.

"I'll have to do measurements first. Then I'll need to check the cost of the timber and let you know." She nodded. What other choice did she have? "I can start now. You go about your business and pretend I'm not here."

Holly didn't think that would even be possible. Marcus Taylor was a large man, at least six feet tall, and was solid. His muscles bulged through his linen shirt, and it took all her effort not to stare. His slightly overgrown hair was as black as the midnight sky and his eyes were the color of the soft flowing chocolate she used in her baking.

"I…I have to collect the other cakes I made at the saloon," she said quietly. "Will you be all right while I'm gone?" She slapped herself mentally. Of course, he would be all right. He was a fireman for goodness sakes. If he could fight fires and save damsels in distress, why wouldn't he be fine in her store on his own? She felt the color flood her cheeks in embarrassment.

When she glanced up, he was grinning. "I think I might survive," he said as he chuckled, basically dismissing Holly from her own store. What a cheek he had. Working with this man was going to be impossible, but as Mrs. Grayson had told her, there wasn't another carpenter for miles around, and her expenses were already blown out. She couldn't afford to bring someone in from one of the surrounding towns.

She hurried out of the kitchen, and snatching the trolley, headed toward the saloon. How on earth would she survive working with this horrid man? The days and weeks ahead would prove to be far beyond difficult. Of that, Holly was certain.

Chapter Two

Marcus had been to the mercantile and obtained the measurements for Holly's new oven. Because she'd bought a second-hand oven previously, one that was already quite old, it presented a problem. The replacement had far different dimensions, and he would need to adjust the cavity it would sit in.

The news would likely be devastating to Holly since it would also affect the cabinets surrounding it. The change was less than a foot in width, but it would make a huge difference to everything else.

He strolled into the kitchen where Holly was decorating cupcakes. He studied her techniques and was rather taken by her skill. "You make it look easy," he said.

"Well, it's not," she snapped.

He studied her. What was her problem? "You really don't like me, do you?" He spoke before he thought and already regretted it.

"First, you snatched me up and stormed out of the store with me in your arms, and then I'm forced ..." She stopped mid-sentence and he wondered what she'd been going to say.

He stared at her. Here was a young woman who almost lost her business, and she was upset because he'd carried her out of a raging fire? If it hadn't been so serious, he might have laughed. "It was the quickest way to get you out," he said quietly, trying to hide his mirth at her indignation. "There was a fire raging in your kitchen. You could have been killed."

Color drained from her face. Perhaps he'd said too much? "But praise the Lord, you were saved." His mind went back to the short time he'd held her in his arms. Despite the danger, he'd enjoyed holding her. Oh, Marcus knew he had no right to feel that way, and he should have put her down far quicker than he had, but the lady did things to him. Made him feel good. A shiver went through him even thinking about it.

"You can't be serious?" Her eyes never left his face and he felt like a moth in a glass jar being scrutinized.

"We know now you were safe, but at the time, we had no idea how much the fire had taken control." He shrugged. "If we hadn't gotten there so quickly, it could have been far worse."

She stared at him for long moments. "Thank you," she said quietly. "I should be far more grateful. I'm sorry." She turned her head away, and Marcus wondered if she was crying, if he'd upset her. No matter, he felt like a heel. His intention hadn't been to upset her, but to make her realize how serious it was and how much danger she'd been in. Now he regretted being so detailed about it.

Holly had been doing it tough since the fire, and he should have been more compassionate toward her. Instead, he had forced his opinions on her and put up a barrier between the two. She went back to her decorating, and he went back to his measurements. Neither one spoke for a long time, and Marcus knew that was his fault.

She suddenly stopped what she was doing and headed out of the kitchen. "Time to open the store," she said quietly, then disappeared out through the swing doors and into the store. He heard a bell tinkle and then muffled conversation. It wasn't long before Holly returned.

She lifted a tray of decorated cupcakes and took them into the store. She returned, this time taking a tray of larger cakes. The bell tinkled several times while she was out there. It was apparent she had a busy and popular store. Despite her obvious dislike of him, Marcus vowed to restore her kitchen to its former glory as quickly as humanly possible.

Marcus was busy pulling off the doors to the cupboards and emptying them out. Holly helped between customers. Neither of them said a word. He was still convinced she didn't like him and wasn't certain it was just over the fire. There seemed to be more. What that was he couldn't put his finger on.

"I'm making coffee," she suddenly said. "You seem like a black coffee man. Am I right?" She smiled at him. A genuine smile this time and not the false one she often wore. Perhaps she was warming to him. Marcus sure hoped so, since he would spend the next few weeks working on her kitchen.

"Yes, black. Two sugars." She grinned, probably because she guessed correctly. "Thank you," he added as he rolled his shoulders. He'd spent most of the morning either pulling supplies out of her cupboards or taking measurements. He really needed a break. Holly had been making slices to fill her display cabinet she'd said, since her oven was out of action. She needed products to sell, and they helped fill a gap. She also had baked goods she'd made at the saloon, but not as many as normal, she'd told him.

She brought his coffee over to the table, along with some iced lemon slices. They looked nice and tasted even better. "These are great," he said. "My grandma used to make them when I was a kid, but they weren't as good as these."

"My grandma taught me to cook," she said quietly. "It was because of her I opened this store. My grandparents left me an inheritance."

The expression she wore was a mixture of sadness and pride. "Well, either way, you're a great cook. You'll make a great wife one day."

She suddenly glared at him, just when she seemed to be warming to him. Had he touched a sore spot? He thought so. She pulled her lips into a tight line and didn't say another word for quite some time. Marcus resisted the urge to chuckle.

"Thank you," he said when he'd finally finished. He carried his mug to the sink and began to wash it.

"Leave it," she said tersely. "I'll do it with the other dishes later."

He didn't know how to take her. Holly was hot and cold, and Marcus was almost certain it was him. She didn't seem to like him at all, and he really didn't know the reason. It surely couldn't relate back to the day of the fire. There had to be more to it. And yet, they hadn't met until that day. It intrigued him as much as it irritated him.

The remainder of the day was spent in near silence, except when there were customers in the store. She closed up at noon and arranged sandwiches for them both after visiting the bakery. She barely spoke a word but placed a mug of black coffee in front of him.

"You don't have to supply a meal," he said, watching her closely.

He thought she'd be happy, but instead, she flinched. "I don't mind," she said firmly. What she really meant, Marcus was certain, was the sooner I get you out of here, the better. Did she hate him that much?

After saying a blessing for their food, they barely spoke. She kept her eyes averted the entire time and didn't once give any indication she was grateful for his help. It was almost enough for him to want to walk out and never come back. But Mrs. Grayson had stressed how important this job was, that Holly had nowhere else to turn. The old lady had been there when his own mother needed help all those years ago, and he would do anything to repay her kindness.

"Thank you for a lovely meal," he said as he stood. "I must get back to work."

She glanced up momentarily. "So must I," she said, and gulped down the last of her coffee. She still looked angry. No, that's not what it was. She seemed...torn. It was as though Holly knew she needed his help but didn't want to accept it.

"I'll be ordering the timber tomorrow," he said suddenly. "It's a pity you don't have a back door. It will have to come through the shop." He felt guilty about doing it, but what choice did he have?

She bit down on her bottom lip. "Do what you have to do," she said firmly. "My customers will understand." She turned then and walked away.

Marcus went back to his work, putting Holly Yates and her moods out of his mind. Even if only for a short time.

Holly was already sick of getting up earlier to use the saloon oven. Oh, she was grateful, beyond thankful for the use of the oven. It was far bigger than hers and certainly more modern. Her new oven would be similar, and she couldn't be happier.

What she didn't like was pushing the trolley through the slush in the freezing weather. Not that her store was much warmer at the moment. Without a working oven, it was quite chilly in her normally pleasant kitchen.

Yesterday, she'd run out of cupcakes, so today, she'd baked an extra dozen. It was certainly a difficult time, but she'd also managed to make cookies today, some birthday cakes, and even managed some Christmas cakes. None of this anywhere equaled her normal output, but she was wasting an incredible amount of time using someone else's oven, as well as their kitchen. She had to bring all her equipment here each day, as well as transport it back to her own kitchen, and it was exhausting.

So now, here she was struggling to control the rickety trolley Hank had resurrected from his dusty basement.

"Good morning."

The voice was far too familiar, and annoying. What was he doing out and about at this hour?

"Let me help," Marcus said, grabbing the other end of the trolley. "I can see you're sliding all over the place."

She should be grateful, she really should, but for some reason, this man grated on her. "Thank you," she said graciously, as though her thoughts didn't go in the complete opposite direction. "I'd hate to lose this lot in the slush.

"That would be a tragedy," he said, lifting the trolley over the step to the *Holly-Berry Cake Shoppe*.

"What are you doing here so early, anyway," she asked as they made their way into the kitchen. With the trolley placed next to the table, Holly removed the cupcakes and placed them, ready to be decorated.

She glanced at him, waiting for an answer.

"I…I knew you'd be struggling with that trolley," he said. "I'm used to getting up early, so it didn't bother me."

He was the perfect gentleman, and she should be ecstatic, but for some reason it grated on her. "You didn't have to do that," she said quietly then turned to leave.

"I'll come with you," he suddenly said. "That's why I'm here, after all."

Holly rolled her shoulders. She should say something. Thank him for his help, but she didn't ask him to come here. Not today, not ever. "Thank you," she finally said, knowing it wasn't his fault. Mrs. Grayson would have coerced him into helping. She was really good at that. Cunning too. Holly wondered what the old lady was up to, because there was no doubt in her mind she was up to something. She always was.

With all her baked goods finally in her kitchen, Holly was able to start work. It was still quite early, and she put the kettle on to boil. "Have you eaten yet?" She glanced across to where he was scribbling numbers on a sheet of paper. No doubt the measurements to her cupboards.

"Not yet. I figured I'd go to the bakery and pick something up later."

"Fiddlesticks," she said, reaching across the table. "I made some egg and bacon pies this morning. It's the first time since the fire." She pulled a paper bag out from a drawer in the table. "I don't have plates, so this is the best I can do."

"You don't have to—"

"—Feed you? I know, but when it's right here, why go buying inferior products?" She grinned then. She meant it as a joke and hoped Marcus took it that way.

She handed him two still-warm pies on top of the bag. "I couldn't," he said, trying to push them away, but she insisted. "Oh, these are good," he said, taking a bite. "I've said it before, and I'll say it again. You're a great cook."

"Don't forget the bit where I'll make someone a great wife," she added flatly.

"Ouch," he said. "I knew I'd upset you when I said it last time." He scowled. "Sorry. I didn't mean anything by it."

She raised her eyebrows. Was that true? Or was he one of those men who thought women belonged barefoot and pregnant at home. Not out working, and certainly not running their own business.

She turned away to make the coffee.

"You don't normally have these in the store, do you?" He sounded rather curious.

"No, I made them especially for our breakfast, but I had a lot of left-over pastry." She shrugged her shoulders. They could always have them for lunch. And would still have several remaining.

"I'm willing to bet you would sell a ton of these. They're delicious."

She studied him. Is it true or is he just saying that, she wondered? "Do you really think so?" Hmmm, it was worth testing his theory.

His mouth too full to speak, he nodded. "I definitely do," he said when his mouth was empty.

She placed the pies on a clean tray then took them into the store. She needed to have something to eat then start decorating. She'd spent far too much time chatting with Marcus. She was beginning to warm to him. Perhaps he was not quite so bad after all.

Chapter Three

Marcus knocked on the window to the saloon's kitchen, startling Holly. She'd taken the last of her baked goods out of the oven. Her earlier creations were almost cool and would be ready to take across to the store on that horrid trolley she now hated.

He was signaling to let him in. He would be no help whatsoever and probably more of a hindrance. But she let him in anyway. "Good morning," she said, already sounding quite weary. "Oh, what is that?" she demanded.

"This?" he asked as though she hadn't pointed to what he held in his hands. "It's a small gift."

She wondered if she looked as surprised as she felt. "A gift? For me?" What on earth was it? It was partly hidden by the door frame.

She held the door wide open and he rolled it in. "For me? Really?" Her heart thudded and she was beyond excited. "Where—"

"—I made it over the past couple of days after I got home," he said. "That thing you're using is damaged, and one of these days it will let you down. I have no doubt of that." He pushed the beautifully crafted and solid trolley toward her. It was at least double the size of Hank's broken-down relic.

"Thank you," she said quietly, trying to fight back tears. "Let me pay you for it."

He stared momentarily. "Then it wouldn't be a gift, would it?"

Marcus was right. It seemed he always was. "I couldn't think of a better gift," she said, tears brimming in her eyes. "Thank you." She stepped forward and hugged him tight. His arms came up around her, and it felt good. She leaned her head against his chest and heard his rapidly beating heart. Did it feel as good for him as it did for her?

She suddenly pulled out of his arms. Holly should never have been so bold and was appalled by her behavior. "Sorry," she said, glancing at him momentarily. "I don't know what came over me."

He grinned. "Don't be sorry. I'm not." He raised his eyebrows at her and it riled her. She was merely thanking him for the wonderful gift he'd given her. Wasn't she?

Of course, she was. As if she would have any sort of relationship with the arrogant, self-centered man standing before her.

Holly stepped back and concentrated on her baking, which is where her focus should always have been. She'd sold out of the egg and bacon pies yesterday, to her surprise, so made far more today. "I hope you don't mind the same thing for breakfast again today," she said. "You were right – the pies were very popular."

He grinned. "What did I tell you?"

Did it always have to be about him? Holly placed as much as she could on the trolley. It held far more than she'd anticipated. "Thank you again," she said, ignoring his comment. "This will make my life a lot easier."

"Even once you have your new oven," he said. Holly knew it was true – even transporting the food within her own store would prove to be far easier. She was certainly looking forward to the day the new oven arrived.

Marcus helped her take her goodies to the store then she unpacked them and they collected more. When everything had been taken to the Holly's store, she put the kettle on for their morning coffee. As much as she complained about him, Marcus was beginning to grow on her. He certainly didn't have to make her that wonderful trolley, but he'd done it out of the kindness of his heart. It seemed Mrs. Grayson was right when she said he was a good man.

To her surprise, there was already a queue of customers waiting outside when Holly opened the store. She hadn't been prepared for the onslaught and was exhausted by the time everyone left. They told her they'd come for the new addition to her range – egg and bacon pies. Dewberry was a small town, and word got around quickly. It was just as well she'd made extras this morning. She'd put some aside for Marcus and herself before placing the rest in the display case, and they'd happily eaten them for breakfast.

She was getting more used to having Marcus around, and felt far more comfortable with him. Her kitchen was a total mess due to the necessary renovations, but at least she knew it was short term. "Time for a break," she said, handing him a coffee. "Take your pick." She waved her hands across the smaller area of the table she'd been relegated to. He had a choice of apple, lemon, and date slices, a variety of cupcakes, and a small selection of cookies. He reached across the table, his hand wavering with indecision. "You're not limited to only one, you know."

He raised his eyebrows and grinned.

Holly handed Marcus a plate she'd brought from home to hold his treasures. One thing she knew for certain, Marcus liked his food. Well, at least he liked her baking.

He raised his eyebrows. "Are you sure? I mean, well, this is your livelihood." And it was, but she couldn't have him fainting on the floor out of starvation, could she?

"I'm sure. Now eat."

Despite her initial dislike of Marcus, he was beginning to get under her skin, and not in a bad way. He'd proven time and again to be an asset to her, and certainly seemed to be a good person. Strange she'd never met him previously.

"Hey," she said after a thought suddenly hit her. "If you're a fireman, how can you be a carpenter?" Why she hadn't thought about it before, she had no idea.

He chuckled. "The fire brigade is volunteer work. We have few fires around here anyway. Carpentry is my real job," he said as he popped a piece of cupcake into his mouth.

Holly sipped her coffee. "How do you know Mrs. Grayson?"

He stared momentarily. "Who doesn't know Mrs. Grayson? To be honest, she helped my family out when I was a little tyke. Well, my mother anyway. Father had been killed in the mines, and we were doing it rough." He shrugged his shoulders. "She makes out she's a tough old bird, but she has the most generous heart."

"She does. Did you know she offered to lend me the money to fix the store?" Holly's heart thudded. Mrs. Grayson was merely an acquaintance. Someone who visited her store regularly and she saw around Dewberry. She couldn't be classified as a close friend. "I told her I'd think about it."

"Like I said, she has a generous heart." The bell over the door tinkled, and Holly put down her coffee. "I'll be back," she said quietly then left. It wasn't long before she returned.

"It's for you. A man who says he has a big pile of timber."

Marcus jumped up from the table. "Wonderful. You might want to cover that food. It could get dusty in here."

Dusty? Holly hadn't thought about that. Better to put them in the display cabinet than take the risk. She was going to do it soon anyway. As she lifted the tray of baked goods, it struck her how considerate Marcus was. He didn't have to warn her about the dust, but had taken the time to help her out. She'd just finished adding all her products to the display case when Marcus and another man began to stroll through the store entrance carrying planks of timber. She held the swing doors open for them and stood out of the way.

As luck would have it, she had no customers while the timber was being carried through the store. Or could it be her customers saw what was going on and kept their distance? Holly strained her neck to see how much room had been taken up in her kitchen with the new materials. True to his word, Marcus had kept it all in one corner of the room. She did, after all, need to work in there each day. Her biggest fear was they would be tripping over each other.

"I'm going to prepare everything before the oven arrives, but it's going to get far messier than you can imagine." He glanced about the room. "Do you mind if I erect a dividing curtain across here," he asked, pointing to the area he had in mind. "That way, the dust will be kept mostly isolated."

"Not at all, thank you. Whatever works." He truly was a thoughtful man. Holly wondered if there was some way she could repay him. She would have to give it some thought.

He went about his business, and Holly continued with her work. She had two birthday cakes to decorate today. They'd been ordered in advance. Plus, she always had at least one extra, just in case. Most days they all sold – being the only cake shop around put her at a distinct advantage despite the fire damage to her beloved store.

"I'll be back later. I need to get some heavy material for the divider."

"Will you be here for lunch?"

He grinned at her. "I wouldn't miss it for the world."

Holly's heart fluttered and it shocked her. There was no reason for it to happen. Marcus Taylor was nothing to her – except for being her carpenter. That was the truth of the matter, and she knew it. Except she didn't. She'd begun having improper thoughts about her carpenter. Things like how she'd liked being held by him. Or what it would be like to be kissed by him. She knew it was wrong, totally wrong, but her heart was telling her otherwise.

The strangest thing was the first time he'd held her, the day of the fire, her thoughts went in the opposite direction. She could only put that down to both fear and the fact she didn't know the man. It still irked her he'd taken advantage of her and not asked her permission.

Now she did know him he was the complete opposite to her first impressions. Although his arrogance still came through at times. She was still fuming over his remark that she'd make someone a good wife.

She heard the bell over the door tinkle and knew he'd gone. It suddenly seemed peaceful. And empty. She'd become so accustomed to having him there and couldn't fathom how she could have survived before – when he wasn't there. The place seemed suddenly barren. Soulless.

It was the strangest feeling, and Holly wasn't sure what to make of it.

The bell tinkled again and her heart raced. Was he back already? That was far quicker than she'd expected. She pushed the swing doors just a fraction to check, only to be met with disappointment. Holly put a false smile on her face and went out to greet Mrs. Grayson. "Good morning," she said far more cheerfully than she felt. "What can I do for you today?"

Her best customer looked about. "Mr. Taylor isn't here?" She looked rather disappointed – much the way Holly felt.

"He'll be back soon. Thank you for sending him to me. He's doing a wonderful job."

The other woman's grin was genuine. "What did I tell you? He is good. Very good." She glanced down into the display cabinet and pondered her selection. "You spoil us, Holly, with such a wonderful selection – even in difficult circumstances." She pointed out her purchases, which were quickly bagged. Instead of leaving, she lingered.

"Was there something else?" It wasn't like her to hang around for long. Mrs. Grayson was usually in and out. Oh, she liked to have a chat at times, but even on those days she didn't talk much, like today, she said what she wanted to say then left. Today was different. She seemed hesitant to get the words out.

"How are you two getting along?" She suddenly blurted the words out. Holly studied her. Was Mrs. Grayson trying to play matchmaker? That was very unlike her, at least to Holly's knowledge.

"Marcus is nice. A real gentleman. We're getting along fine." Her customer nodded her head. "Most of the time, anyway."

Mrs. Grayson pursed her lips. "What did he do? He's not the most subtle person I know."

"Nothing much, not really. Told me I'd make a good wife someday."

The other woman chuckled. "That sounds like him." She reached over and patted Holly's hand. "The problem is, he is rather traditional, old fashioned, and you my dear, are an independent woman." Without another word, she took her purchases from Holly and turned away. "I shall see you again soon." And then she was gone.

Holly knew she was right. She liked to think of herself as being a modern woman who was fiercely independent. Most men she knew were not all right with that. She wondered what Marcus thought. For some strange reason, his opinion meant a lot to her.

Chapter Four

The past week had been rather tedious. Holly had been relegated to a restricted area to carry out her decorating, and the noise level had become almost unbearable. Marcus was hidden behind that unsightly curtain, but she knew it was for a reason – to protect her products from the dust. If it weren't for the curtain he'd erected, dust would be flying everywhere, and she'd have no safe place to do her decorating.

It was difficult enough baking at the saloon, let alone having to do everything else. Besides the fact it was out of the question. Once the saloon's cook came in to do his preparation, she had no choice but to leave.

She felt blessed to have been offered that wonderful kitchen to work in, and would make the best of a bad situation.

Finally, the sawing stopped. She took a big restorative breath. Perhaps a break would do them both good. It seemed silly, but she'd missed him, although he was still in the room. The thing was you couldn't to talk to a person hidden behind a screen. Nor did you get to joke with them, or see their facial expressions. Or even touch them. It felt like forever since they'd shared those things, but the fact was, it only a matter of days.

"I'm making coffee," she called out as she checked the kettle that was already near boiling. Holly pulled the mugs from the cupboard and prepared them for their beverages.

"Sounds good." His voice was muffled through the curtain but was still legible. She could hear him brushing off the dust moments before he appeared. "You have no idea how much I've been looking forward to this."

Did he mean the coffee, or spending time with her? Holly's heart was pounding – as crazy as it sounded, she felt like she was meeting up with a long-lost friend. She was in a way; Marcus had been hidden in his own little domain for days. "How much longer until the curtain can come down?" She glanced across at him, and he appeared startled.

Then he grinned. "Did you miss me?" She knew it was a joke, but he had guessed correctly. That was exactly how she felt, and it made her heart flutter now. Did he feel the same way? She shook herself mentally. Of course he didn't. Marcus Taylor was certain to have a girlfriend tucked away somewhere. Although Mrs. Grayson hadn't mentioned one. But still…

The kettle boiled, interrupting her thoughts. Holly made the coffee and placed a mug in front of him. She reached for the plate of assorted treats she'd put together and placed them on the table. Marcus reached for them as she pulled away, and their hands touched. It felt like a bolt of lightning ran up her arm and she quickly pulled her hand away. Marcus studied her. Did he feel it too?

He continued to stare momentarily then again reached for something to eat. "You're a good woman," he told Holly, his gaze never leaving hers. "You're an excellent cook too." He took a bite of the lemon-flavored cupcake with its tangy lemon icing. It was one of her specialties, and Holly always sold a ton of those. "Mmmm, this is good."

"Help yourself to more," she said as he took the last bite. She reached out to grab an apple slice, and their hands touched again. This time, instead of pulling away, she left her hand right where it was. Marcus held her hand in his. It felt good, nice, and she was happy to leave it right where it was until she realized they shouldn't be doing this.

She glanced up and he stared into her eyes. "You have beautiful eyes," he said gently. "They are the color of marble."

Holly blinked. "Marble?" That didn't sound romantic at all. "My eyes look like slabs of marble?" Now she frowned.

"I didn't mean it like that. You have pretty eyes, beautiful in fact. I could stare into them all day." He let go of her hand and took another treat. "Unfortunately, I have work to do, and my boss is counting on me to have all this ready in time for her new oven's arrival."

That made her grin. "Not long now, I hope." The thought of her new oven made Holly incredibly happy. Finally, she would be able to cook in her own kitchen again. But on the other hand, Marcus' job would then be finished and she may never see him again. She suddenly felt hollow. The thought of not having Marcus in her life made her sad.

She wondered how he felt. Would he miss her, or was she just another job to him? Most likely the latter, Holly decided. He didn't seem the sort of man who would be lonely for long and probably had women flocking to his door.

He gulped down the last of his coffee. "That was great, thanks. I have to get back to work now." She followed him to the dividing curtain and craned her neck to check it out. What he'd done so far looked wonderful. Very functional, and she couldn't wait for it to be finished. "There's still a lot to do," he explained. That lifted her spirits quite a bit. "I've done the base for the oven, as you can see, since that got the most damage and everything had to be built around it." He ran his hands over the surrounds of the wooden cavity, and Holly wanted to do the same.

Before she could do something so forward, she checked herself. What would Marcus think of her if she did such a thing? She didn't dare think. "It looks amazing. I'm so glad Mrs. Grayson sent you to me."

He lifted one eyebrow. "You do realize she has an ulterior motive, right?" A small smile formed on his mouth. "She's a cunning old bird. Nice, but crafty."

"I knew it, I just knew it," Holly said, clapping her hands together. Although why she felt elated knowing the devious old lady was matchmaking, she wasn't sure. Perhaps because it confirmed her suspicions. "She asked about you last time she came into the store."

He chuckled. "She asks about you whenever I see her. I knew she was up to something."

Holly scowled. "You think it's funny? Do you like her meddling in your love life? Because I don't."

Marcus straightened and stared at her. "You have a love life? Lucky you." He chuckled again. "We should find a way to put her back in her place."

She had no idea what that could be but agreed with Marcus. Mrs. Grayson needed to be taught a lesson. She needed to keep her matchmaking ideas to herself.

"Back to work," Marcus declared. "I will see you later." He pulled the curtain across, and the hammering began again.

Holly already missed him but knew she shouldn't.

With her picnic basket packed, minus the food, Holly strolled from home to her store. Today, she would surprise Marcus. They would have a picnic lunch in the park – just the two of them. When she baked this morning, she would include items they could have for their meal. Chicken pies would be nice for a change, and she'd make enough to sell in the store. As awful as the fire was, in some ways it had been a blessing.

She now had a far bigger range of food for sale and sold out quickly each time. Annabelle at the bakery might not be happy, but she had a roaring business too. With her husband helping, they were able to produce far more items to sell than Holly. She shrugged her shoulders. That was the way things went, and there was nothing she could do about it.

Holly unlocked the door to the *Holly-Berry Cake Shoppe* and placed her basket in the cupboard under the sink. Marcus wouldn't see it there, so the surprise wouldn't be spoiled. She collected up all her ingredients as she had done every other day and placed them on the wonderful trolley Marcus had made for her. It had made her life so much easier. Another reason to be thankful for having him in her life.

By the time she was ready to take her first trolley load of goodies to the store, Marcus had arrived. "The aroma is amazing in here," he said as he helped her load the trolley. He was right, and she never stopped loving it. Holly recalled it was one of the things that had drawn her to baking in the first place. She loved the mix of aromas that came from her grandmother's kitchen, and it compelled her to do her own baking.

"That's different," Marcus said, pointing to the chicken pies. "Or am I mistaken?"

She smiled. "No mistake. They're chicken pies. I've still got egg and bacon pies, but thought this would be nice for a change."

He nodded then helped her move the trolley across to her own store. "It does sound delicious." They reached the store and he unlocked the door, then Marcus lifted it over the step as he'd done every other day. What Holly would do without him she didn't know. Of course, by then her new oven would be installed and working, and she wouldn't be lugging her baked goods over to her store each day.

Still, she didn't want to think of life without him. Holly wondered when she'd let him get under her skin, into her mind. And into her heart.

"I hope you're going to be around for lunch today," she told him without elaborating.

He glanced up, a grin on his face. "I'm always around for your baking," he said. She slipped the items onto the table and covered them up then they returned to the saloon for the next round. "What did you have in mind?"

Should she tell him? Holly really wanted it to be a surprise. He studied her. Sometimes, she thought he was trying to see all the way into her soul. "It's a surprise," she said then turned away. He reached out and gently grabbed her arm, turning her back to face him.

"You can't say that and leave it at that." Although he tried to sound annoyed, she knew he was joking with her, as he often did.

She laughed. "If you want the surprise, you'll have to wait. Otherwise, it's not a surprise."

He pulled her closer. "What can I do to get you to tell me?" They were so close she could feel his breath on her face. Not that she didn't like it, but she knew they shouldn't be like this, especially since they were alone.

"There's nothing." She looked up into his face and his eyes pierced her. She was certain he was going to kiss her, and she stiffened, which didn't make sense since it was what she'd dreamed about. She put her hands to his chest to push him away and felt his quickened heartbeat, and Holly knew they were both feeling the same way. "Marcus, I…"

She didn't get to finish the sentence as his face moved closer to hers and then he kissed her. Right there in the middle of the saloon kitchen. What if the cook arrived early? Then they'd be compromised. As if she'd made it happen, the door handle rattled and the door flew open. Marcus jumped back and grinned.

"Sorry, Sherman," Holly said breathlessly, heat creeping up her face. "I'll be out of your way in just a moment."

She began stacking her items but noticed his gaze go from Marcus to Holly, then he winked at Marcus. Hot fury engulfed her. How dare he insinuate…It was then she realized he was right. The thing Sherman had thought happened, actually had. It was as much her fault as it was Marcus's, and she was annoyed. With the both of them.

"Take your time," the cook said. "I'm early anyway." He stared at the trolley then turned to

Marcus. "Did you make this trolley? It's very impressive."

"I did. The one Hank lent to Holly was in a pretty bad state."

It was a good distraction, Holly decided. Perhaps Sherman would forget their little, er, indiscretion. But probably not.

"Could you make one for me? For the saloon? We'll pay for it, of course." Holly watched as he stared Marcus down, silently urging him to agree.

"Of course, but it might not be for a week or two."

Sherman nodded then slapped the other man on the back. "I understand. You have your hands full repairing Holly's kitchen."

"Thanks, Sherman," Holly said as they left to return to her own store.

"That was close," Marcus said as she closed the door behind them.

"If by close you mean caught, then yes it was," she said, then grinned. She wondered if Marcus would kiss her again. This time, she'd like to have time enough to enjoy it.

Holly flipped the closed sign on the shop door. It was time for their lunch break. The sun was shining, although, it was still chilly outside. She'd noticed a few flurries over the course of the morning. Not that she should be surprised; it was almost Christmas after all. Soon their days would be nothing but snow, and they would freeze without a warm coat.

She would be pleased to have her new oven installed, and not just because she'd be working in her own kitchen again, but also for the warmth it would produce. Hopefully, only a few more days until her pride and joy arrived; it filled her heart with happiness.

Marcus was still hammering on the other side of the curtain, and she pulled the basket out from under the sink. Holly filled it with items for their lunch, and placed a bottle of water and some mugs in the basket too.

"Time for lunch," she called loudly to make herself heard over the hammering.

The noise suddenly stopped. "Sounds good to me," he said, and Holly imagined him stretching himself out as he always did after he stopped working. It was a sight to behold as his muscles rippled. She knew she shouldn't feel this way, but Holly loved to watch it.

Now he would be flicking the sawdust from his clothes and running his hands down his firm thighs. Her heart fluttered just thinking about it.

Suddenly the curtain opened wide, and heat flooded her face. She shouldn't be thinking such things about her worker. That's what he was, and Marcus himself said so when he'd called her his boss. It brought her back to reality. "This is my surprise," she said, holding up the basket in front of him. "I thought we'd have a picnic before the weather got too bad." She glanced out the window to make sure it was still fine, and thankfully, it was. Otherwise they'd have an inside picnic. That would certainly be different.

"It sounds wonderful," he said as he pulled on his thick coat.

Holly did the same and they were off. "There's a pergola where we can sit and eat out of the weather. It's not very far from here."

"I know where it is," he said. "The surrounding park is quite pretty if memory serves."

Holly hooked her arm through his, but not before Marcus took the basket from her. She was looking forward to their special time together.

It didn't take long to arrive at the pergola and settle themselves in to eat. Holly spread a picnic blanket across the floor as it was damp on the grass from the flurries. It wasn't ideal, but it would still be fun.

She glanced up to see Marcus grinning. "What?" She had no idea what was so funny.

"Do you normally have a picnic *inside* the pergola?"

He had a point, but the weather was a little uncooperative. "Do you want to fight the flurries?" He waved a hand in the air, and she took it that he really didn't care. She snatched up the blanket in a huff and moved outside. It was chilly, as she'd predicted, but it wasn't too cold as to be uncomfortable.

Marcus followed her outside with the basket, a smile on his face. "This was a lovely idea," he said. "and I do like surprises."

After Holly emptied the food onto the blanket, he studied the offering. "This looks great. You've included some chicken pies too."

The smile on his face filled her with warmth. How was it that this man was able to fill her with joy over the smallest of things? Holly poured them each some water and passed him an empty plate. "Help yourself. There's plenty of food, as you can see."

He reached over and grabbed one of the chicken pies. They were still slightly warm since Holly had kept them wrapped for that very reason. "They're delicious, Holly. No matter what you make, it's tasty. You have the knack, that's for certain."

"I can't wait for my new oven to arrive," she said, avoiding his compliment. It wasn't that she didn't like praise, but sometimes it felt unwarranted. She leaned in to take one of the pies, unaware Marcus would do the same thing. Their faces were just inches apart. More importantly, their lips were close, and she wanted so badly to kiss him. To feel his lips on hers again. Their kiss this morning was nice but was far from long enough. If Sherman hadn't interrupted them...

Marcus reached out and pulled her closer, and soon their lips were touching. He brushed his warm mouth across hers and a thrill went through her. Despite the distance between them, he pulled her closer, pushing the food aside. Holly was both happy and concerned. What if someone she knew saw them? She shuddered.

"Are you cold?" Marcus' voice startled her.

He began to pull his coat off, but she stopped him. "It's not that. What if someone sees us?"

"What if they do," he said. It was a statement, not a question, and Holly immediately knew he didn't care. "I have feelings for you," he said.

She felt the same, but did she dare admit it? They were employer and employee after all. Never before had Holly allowed her personal feelings to interfere with a work relationship. But never before had someone like Marcus worked for her. And never before had she felt this way. It was a dilemma she needed to resolve, and she hadn't helped by bringing him out here for an intimate picnic.

Her head leaned against his chest, and she felt far more comfortable than she should. His arms came up around her back, as though he was ensuring she didn't leave. The thought had entered her mind, but since she instigated this rendezvous, she couldn't up and go.

"I don't know what to do." Marcus stared into her eyes as she said the words, and his expression became somber. "I mean, well, you work for me," she said sadly.

"That can't change until the job is done." He studied her now, and she wanted to squirm, but he had a firm grip on her. "There is no one else in Dewberry who can do the work. Besides, it shouldn't change things between us."

"I really like you, Marcus," she said quietly. "More than like you, but you know what people around here are like. We have to keep our distance or tongues will be wagging." She glanced up at him pleadingly. It was not his reputation that would be sullied, but hers. No one would judge Marcus, but they would certainly judge Holly, and her business would suffer because of it.

His chocolate colored eyes studied her. His hand came up to her cheek. "You're right," he said gently. "I've been selfish, and I'm sorry." He released his grip on her and she scurried to the other side of the blanket, relieved he agreed.

She pulled the food back between them, and again reached for one of the chicken pies. Her appetite was lost, but Holly ate anyway. She needed to keep up her strength for the days ahead. How she was going to keep her distance from Marcus, she had no idea. Once the oven was installed and his work was finished, they would go their separate ways.

Her mind told her it was the right thing to do, but her heart told her it was totally wrong.

Marcus relished the feel of Holly on his arm. Their walk back to the store was in silence – they both had things to consider. For him, it wasn't a problem that he was working for Holly, but for her it was a whole different ball game. It was always the woman that received the tongue lashing, not the man. But if people thought she'd been compromised, her business could be in jeopardy.

He glanced sideways at her. Holly held herself stiffly and her face looked tense. It didn't seem such a big thing at first, but if things got out of hand, the entire town of Dewberry would be up in arms. He would marry Holly in a heartbeat, but he was convinced she would refuse on principal. She was probably right – why should she be forced to marry simply because people thought she might be compromised?

But he was getting ahead of himself.

The truth of the matter was he was falling in love with her. Did Holly feel the same? He had absolutely no idea, but she certainly hadn't refused his advances when he kissed her in the saloon kitchen. Not until Sherman walked in anyway. The pink blotches that tinged her face were sweet. The look of embarrassment on her face was priceless. He'd kiss her again in a heartbeat.

"Are you all right," he asked quietly.

She turned her head to face him. "Of course. Why wouldn't I be?"

So that's how it was going to be? She was going to conveniently forget what happened between them. Twice now. His heart fluttered. Marcus wasn't sure he could survive being in the same room with her day after day and not being able to hold her in his arms. At least with a curtain between them, it wasn't quite so difficult, and he had his work to concentrate on.

He glanced across at her again. She held herself rigid, while pretending everything was fine. Nothing was. Marcus had never felt this way before and was convinced he never would again. He had to get through the next couple of weeks, and once his work was done, he would begin to court her. That's what he should have done from the beginning – he could see that now. He'd done everything back to front; first he'd held her in his arms when that should come much later. He never was one for convention, but if he were to win Miss Holly Yates over, that's exactly what he needed to do.

Chapter Five

It was an exciting day. Holly's oven was arriving and would be installed. Due to this monumental event, the store would open two hours later than normal. It was not something she relished, but the alternative was to close for the day.

Men would be wandering in and out of the building, taking her oven inside in the pieces it arrived in. Then it would be assembled. Marcus had already built the cabinet that would surround it, and it was beautiful. Her entire kitchen was far better than it had been before.

The only downside to all this was that Marcus' job was nearly done. Soon, he would be gone, and her heart would be empty once more. It had been difficult keeping her distance, but she'd made a decision and had stuck to it, no matter how much it broke her heart.

With all the excitement going on around her, Holly still had a shop to run. She'd done all her baking at the saloon as usual, and Marcus had helped her bring it across. Today, she would do her decorating out in the shop, something she never did. With all the activity in the kitchen, there was no choice. She'd retrieved all her decorating ingredients and tools and taken them into the shop. It would be difficult, but she could do it, she knew she could.

"They'll be here soon. Are you ready for this?" Marcus stood on the other side of the counter watching her preparations.

"Yes. No." She glanced down at the cupcakes. "I'm really not sure."

"Keep out of the way so you don't get hurt and you should be fine. I'll keep an eye out."

He was her protector now? Keep an eye out indeed – she was quite capable of looking after herself but thought the better of saying so. "Thank you, Marcus. I should be fine back here."

As if it was pre-planned, a wagon pulled up out the front of the store, and three men jumped down. One of them waved to Marcus and he waved back. "This is it," he said. "Your oven is here."

He sounded as unsure about the whole situation as she did, his voice quivering as he spoke. Once his work was finished here, there was no need for them to see each other again. The thought broke her heart, but it had to be.

"Morning, Missus," the scruffy looking man said, touching a finger to his hat. "Where's this thing goin'?"

"Follow me," Marcus said, and the man followed him into the kitchen. She heard muffled voices, which were raised from time to time, then both men stormed outside without a word. It was enough to put terror into her heart. Was there a problem with her new oven? Holly certainly hoped not. She continued to decorate her cakes while a heated discussion transpired outside. Marcus looked quite agitated; she'd never seen him like that before. Now she was really worried.

He glanced up and saw her watching then came inside. "They say they aren't installing it," he said, barely holding onto his anger. "Reckons they were only paid to deliver it, and then they're leaving."

"Oh my!" Holly's heart pounded. "What do we do now?"

Marcus frowned. "Where's the paperwork from the mercantile? I need to check it out."

She located the paperwork quickly and handed it over. Holly watched closely as Marcus read through it. He suddenly pointed at something in the fine print. "Here," he said. "Installation is included in the price you paid. Those mong…" He glanced up at her and suddenly stopped talking. "They're trying to get out of doing what you've paid them to do."

Holding tightly to the paperwork, he stormed out of the store and confronted the men. An argument ensued, but soon afterwards, they began to carry her oven inside, bit by bit. Perhaps it would be installed today after all.

Holly busied herself with her decorating, trying not to be distracted by the workers. She tried not to worry, knowing Marcus was overseeing the whole thing for her. What she would do without him she didn't know. Sure, she was paying him to do a job, but this was not part of it. What he'd done today went far above what he needed to do. Without him, she would have a pile of metal sitting in her kitchen, and not a working oven. At this very moment, Marcus had them testing it, ensuring it worked correctly. He wouldn't allow them to leave until they proved to him it was working as it should. He'd told them so in no uncertain terms.

As she added the last part of the decoration to the requested birthday cake, she leaned back and sighed. It had been a long morning, but it would be worth it in the end. She'd keep telling herself that. Holly glanced at the clock – only another fifteen minutes and her store was due to open. Already, customers were lingering outside the store. She glanced about; the floor needed sweeping, and those wretched men were still in her kitchen.

Marcus ducked his head around the swing door. "Got a minute? Come and check it out." He was gone as quickly as he'd arrived.

She put the cake in the display cabinet then wiped her hands on her apron. Her heart pounded, which was silly, she knew. It was an oven, nothing life changing. Although to Holly, a new oven would be transformational.

She pushed the door open and simply stared. It was there in all its glory; her shiny, bright wood-fired oven. Marcus strolled over to her, pride written all over his face, and slid an arm around her waist. "It's...beautiful," she said quietly, overwhelmed with emotion.

His arm tightened, and he lifted a hand to caress her cheek. "And it's working," he said, stepping forward. "Feel the heat coming from this." He opened the door and heat rushed out.

Holly fought back tears. She knew she shouldn't feel so emotional over an oven, but she couldn't help it. So much had happened since the fire, including meeting Marcus. His work here was almost done, and she was certain that was adding to her emotional state.

"Thank you," she whispered. She glanced across at the three men who'd tried to cheat her, and Holly's heart hardened, but only for a moment. She silently prayed to find forgiveness toward them. They had to live with themselves for what they tried to do to her, but Holly wouldn't allow their actions to make her bitter. She looked up at Marcus and smiled. It would be far easier from now on. Life would get back to normal, back to what it used to be.

Marcus pulled her closer. It was as though he knew his support was needed now more than ever. Warmth flooded her, and she snuggled against him.

"If that's it, we're off," the man who appeared to be in charge said. "We've been here longer than we should have been."

Marcus grimaced. "If you'd done the right thing to begin with, you'd be gone now." The other man looked annoyed, but what Marcus said was true. They'd tried to cheat her. She'd be sure to let Jess Andrews at the mercantile know what had occurred so he would follow up. It made him look bad, but Holly knew Jess had no hand in this.

The men gathered up their tools and left. Holly's relief was palpable. She'd had a bad feeling about them from the moment they'd arrived and was grateful for Marcus' intervention. Without him, she'd be in serious trouble right now. Marcus followed them out, and Holly reached for her broom. The kitchen was a mess, but that could wait. Her shop was about to open and the floor in there was filthy. She couldn't have customers coming in and seeing that – what would they think of her? She quickly swept the floor then ran the mop over it. She wiped down the countertop and was soon ready.

It felt strange baking in her own kitchen again. It had been weeks since she'd done so, and Holly had gotten used to the saloon kitchen. She was grateful for their concession to her under the circumstances, and wanted to find a way to thank them. Saloon owner Hank Spencer would have none of it. Marcus had made Sherman not one, but two trolleys, and refused to take any money for them. It was a thank you gift, he'd said. He didn't need to do that, and Holly was more than happy to pay him for them, but again, he refused.

She glanced across at her kitchen table. The one she'd worked at since her little shop opened. The one Marcus had restored back to its former glory. She'd never been so happy to work in her own little space.

"I'll be out of your hair soon," Marcus said as he began packing up the tools he'd used to transform her workspace over the past weeks.

Holly swallowed. Would she ever see him again, or would he be gone from her life forever? The thought had her heart pounding. As much as she'd demanded they couldn't have a relationship while they worked together, it seemed he was about to walk away. That prospect shattered her heart.

Holly stared at the jelly tarts sitting on her work bench. The *Holly-Berry Cake Shoppe* had been her entire life since the doors opened. Marcus had made her realize there was more to life than a store. That people were important too, but that was all about to change. He was going to leave, and there wasn't a thing she could do about it.

The pot on the stove was bubbling away and demanded her attention, but Holly's interest was focused on Marcus. "You going to get that?" He pointed at the large pot with its boiling water and rattling lid, and she forced her attention to the tiny Christmas puddings in the large boiler.

Using kitchen towels, she removed the lid then carefully removed each tiny pudding. They needed to cool before she could do anything with them. This close to Christmas, she added more festive treats to her range, and these were only the beginning. Soon, she would make Christmas cakes, shortbread cookies, and mince pies. Not to mention full sized Christmas puddings and gingerbread.

Many of the town's women did their own baking, but equally as many didn't. Busy with children and husbands, some helping with their family's business, Holly's offerings were the next best thing.

What she loved most was the scrumptious aromas her baking elicited. She glanced across at her oven and sighed. It was wonderful to be back where she belonged with an oven that cooked to perfection. She breathed in the fragrance of home-baked produce and felt like she'd come home. Her kitchen was her safe place, the place she knew everything would be all right. The fire had ejected her from that place of safety, and she never wanted to go there again.

"Are you all right, Holly?"

She startled at the sound of Marcus' voice. She was so lost in her own thoughts she'd forgotten he was still there. "I'm fine. I was thinking about everything that transpired over these past awful weeks." Her heart was still pounding from the fright she'd had.

"Not everything about it was terrible," he said. "I can think of a few wonderful things that happened." He grinned, and she scowled at him.

Yes, there were some great things that came out of the tragedy, but they would soon end when he walked out the shop door for the last time. "I'm sure you can," she said then turned back to her work. It was going to be hard enough saying goodbye to him. Why did he have to prolong it?

His toolbox rattled as Marcus snapped it shut. Holly stared at it. So, this was it, the end of their association, their friendship. She didn't want it to end, but it wasn't up to her.

"I'm off then," he said gingerly, lingering near the door. Was he waiting for her to stop him? As much as it pained her to see him go, she couldn't and wouldn't ask him to stay. That had to be his choice, and his alone.

"Thanks for everything," she managed to say through unshed tears.

He stared at her momentarily then opened his mouth to say something, but snapped his mouth shut as the bell over the door tinkled. He hurried out of the kitchen without another word.

"Ah, Mr. Taylor. How is Miss Yate's kitchen going?" She would know Mrs. Grayson's voice anywhere.

"It's finished," she heard him answer. "I was just leaving."

"That's it? You're not—"

"—My work is done," he said abruptly, then Holly heard the door slam closed. She swallowed back her emotions and went out to see to her customer, preparing herself for the interrogation she knew would follow.

"Holly, there you are, my dear." Mrs. Grayson looked unusually sad. "Marcus has left, I see." She studied Holly, and Holly finally knew the older woman was disappointed they'd parted ways.

"Yes, my kitchen is finished. He did a wonderful job, too. See for yourself." She didn't normally let customers into her store, but today she made an exception.

Mrs. Grayson popped her head through the swing doors. "Oh, it's lovely. I told you he was good."

Holly smiled. "Yes, you did. Thank you for sending him to me." Despite their separation, she truly was grateful for the other woman's assistance in getting her little store back to normal.

Mrs. Grayson pursed her lips. "And that's it? You're happy for him to leave?"

Holly's heart thudded. What choice did she have? "He's finished his—"

"—So Marcus said," she near snapped. "What is wrong with you two? You are perfectly matched. Did you not like him?" Now she frowned.

"Like him? The man is irritatingly perfect." Holly slapped her hands to her mouth. If only she'd thought before speaking.

A sly smile appeared on the older woman's face. "So, you do like him. Wonderful," she said, rubbing her hands together. "Did he at least kiss you?"

Now her customer was going a bit far, but before she could think straight, Holly answered truthfully. "More than once," she said quietly. "But I put a stop to it. He was my employee after all."

"You are a foolish young woman." Mrs. Grayson suddenly turned on her heel and left the store. Holly spied her sitting on the wooden bench out in the courtyard. She was chatting with none other than Marcus Taylor.

Chapter Six

The past days had gone slowly, even more so because Marcus was no longer working nearby. Holly had become far too used to the captivating young man for her own good, despite what Mrs. Grayson told her.

She loaded the last of the cupcakes into the display cabinet then reached for the mini puddings. She'd decorated each one with fake holly leaves she'd made herself and smiled with pride. They were one of her best festive offerings and always sold out quickly.

She was taking orders for the full-sized puddings and would begin making those soon. Christmas cake orders were flowing in as well. It was going to be a busy couple of weeks, but it was nothing new; Holly did this same thing every year. At least her new oven had arrived in time for all this festive cooking. The thought made her smile.

She glanced up as she felt eyes on her, only to find Marcus standing outside the door. Why he was hesitating, she had no idea. He reached his hand out and held the handle, his eyes never leaving her. What was he doing? Why didn't he open the door and come inside? She didn't know the answer to either question and hurried around to the other side of the counter and opened the door wide. "What are you doing standing out there in the cold?" She reached out and brushed snow from his shoulder and instantly regretted it. His touch was enough to send her heart to fluttering.

Marcus reached up and covered her hand with his own. A shiver went through her despite his gloves being between them. It occurred to Holly she didn't even have to touch his bare skin to elicit a reaction. It bothered her that he was able to induce such an effect, but warmth filled her at his mere presence.

He gripped her hand and she pulled him inside. It was freezing out there without a coat, and since she hadn't planned to be out in the snow, she now shivered. He lifted his arms and wrapped her in his warmth. Holly immediately molded into him. She knew she shouldn't, but she'd missed him these past days; far more than she'd imagined possible.

Finally, he pulled away. "I could stay like this for hours," he said quietly, then pulled his coat off. "I thought we could talk, about…us." He stared into her eyes and his gaze never left her.

She studied him for long moments. "There is no us," she said quietly, wishing things could be different. He opened his mouth to protest when the bell on the door jingled.

"Hello Mrs. Halicourt. What can I do for you today?" The customer told Holly her requirements then left, but not before she took a good long look at Marcus then smiled.

"Where were we?" he asked. "Oh, yes…"

The bell jingled again. "Oh, Mrs. Herbert," Holly said. "I have your order ready." She reached under the counter and pulled out a box with the customer's birthday cake. "See you next time," Holly said as Marcus held the door open for the woman to leave.

He stared at the door as though daring another customer to walk through it. That's exactly what happened, and he wasn't happy. "Mrs. Carson," he said, then turned to Holly. "I'll pick you up at six for supper," he said, then pulled his coat on and left the store.

"Oh, how lovely," Mrs. Carson said. "A lovely young man, that Marcus Taylor. I'm sure you'll have a wonderful evening." Holly bagged up the customer's purchases and handed them over. "I heard you two were stepping out," Mrs. Carson said as she was leaving.

Holly knew exactly where that rumor would have come from. They were being set up, and Mrs. Grayson was behind it all. Holly was fuming – she was very fond of the elderly lady but wished she would mind her own business.

The door opened again, and this time it was Noelle Jenkins from *Book Time*, the Dewberry bookstore. Finally, a friendly face. "Oh, Noelle. It is sooo good to see you!" Holly didn't mean to be so exuberant in her greeting but felt as though she was caught in the midst of a conspiracy.

Noelle stopped suddenly, gazing at Holly as though she was seeing someone entirely different. "Are you all right, Holly? You look quite flustered." The two had been friends for as long as Holly could remember. If she were honest with herself, Noelle was the only person she felt she could confide in.

"Mrs. Grayson – she's trying to match me up with Marcus Taylor." She rolled her eyes as though it was such a terrible situation to be in.

Noelle leaned her elbows on the countertop and had a dreamy expression on her face. "I wouldn't mind her matching me up with Marcus."

You can have him then, Holly almost blurted out, but she liked him too much to pass on him just like that. She hadn't gotten to know him terribly well over the past weeks. They were both working and didn't have a lot of time to socialize.

"I heard you're going to supper tonight." Noelle raised her eyebrows at Holly, trying to elicit further juicy gossip.

"What? Who told you that?" She rolled her eyes again. "Don't tell me – it was Mrs. Carson. She was in the store when Marcus asked me out. Well, told me we were going." She scowled now; she hadn't actually accepted his invitation.

Noelle frowned at her. "You're not going to refuse, are you? There are plenty of us standing in line if you pass him over."

She might be Holly's friend, but that didn't mean she could jump in and take her…what was he? Marcus wasn't courting her; they weren't engaged, so he wasn't a fiancée. Quite frankly, Holly wasn't sure what he was to her. Merely an interested party at this point. Besides, Holly didn't have a claim on him. Did she?

"Is it really that bad?" Noelle was studying her then glanced down into the display cabinet when she saw

Holly had noticed her staring. She cleared her throat then suddenly acted like a customer and not a friend. "I need something for book club tonight. What do you suggest?"

"There are still plenty of cupcakes, or there's a pound cake. Oh, I have a gingerbread loaf too. You really should come earlier in the day to have more choice. Or order ahead."

"I really should," Noelle said, frowning with indecision. "I'll take eight of those cupcakes," she finally said. "They do look delicious."

Holly placed them in a small box and added them to Noelle's business account. It was nice to be busy, but sometimes a break would be nice.

"Thanks," Noelle called as she hurried out the door. "Enjoy supper with Mr. Dreamy."

Holly sighed at Noelle's words. It wasn't like she really had a choice.

Glancing at the clock, she noticed it was getting late. She liked to have the kitchen totally clean by the end of the day, ready for the next morning's baking. Before she tackled that, she swept the shop floor. It wasn't too bad, but the weather conditions meant dirt and flurries messed up the shop entrance. There was no point mopping it now; she'd do that in the morning before the store opened.

Holly hurried into the kitchen and poured a small amount of boiling water in a tub, ready to scrub down the table. It was already clean, but she liked to leave her kitchen spotless. She glanced across at her new oven. It needed a wipe over too. After tackling the kitchen, there was only the used trays to wash. She cleaned, dried, and put them away. No matter how much she cleaned, there was always more to do.

Before she knew it, the bell over the door tinkled, and Marcus stood with his head ducked around the swing doors. "Ready?"

Oh, she was ready to go to supper with him, but Holly wasn't certain she was ready for the conversation he wanted to have.

"I'll have the fish pie, thanks, Merry." With both their orders now taken and Merry out of earshot, Holly settled back against the padded seat. Marcus studied her from across the table, his gaze so intense it made Holly uncomfortable. Her mouth was dry; so dry it felt as though her tongue was stuck to her mouth. She reached out and took a sip of water.

"I've missed you," Marcus said as he reached out and covered her free hand. She didn't answer. Instead, Holly waited for him to continue. "I know it's only been a matter of days, but it feels like a lifetime to me." She still didn't speak but squirmed in her seat. "What about you?"

Was he asking if she missed him? Oh, she missed him all right. Sometimes, it felt like a piece of her had been wrenched from her very being. "I, uh…"

"It's all right," he said quickly. "You don't have to say anything." He suddenly looked sad and Holly knew she'd upset him.

"Honestly," she said quietly, "I've missed you more than I ever thought possible. You've been a big part of my life for weeks, and now my kitchen seems so…empty." She stared down into her lap. Glancing up, she noticed he was grinning like a Cheshire cat.

His hand crawled across the table to hers, and he squeezed her hand. "That's the best news I've ever heard," he said. Holly stared at him. "I was worried you were glad to see the back of me." He studied her now. He did that a lot, Holly finally realized. Was it something he kept for only her, or did he do that to everyone?

"I think you're seeing far more into it than there is," she said. Before he had an opportunity to speak, their food arrived. "Thanks, Merry," she said quietly as she glanced up.

"We'll eat first then talk," Marcus told her, then reached out and grabbed her hand. He said a blessing then tucked into his food.

As always, the food was good. Merry had inherited *Ma's Kitchen* when her mother passed. Merry had practically grown up in the little diner and was no stranger to how the food here was made and how the diner should be run.

When they finished eating, Marcus ordered hot beverages and dessert. They chatted about the various activities happening around Dewberry, but he refused to talk about the topic at hand until they'd finished eating. As Holly took her last mouthful of tea, he began again. "So, as I was saying earlier, or at least trying to say," He stared into her eyes. "I've missed you far too much, as I knew I would."

Her heart thudded. Was Marcus saying what she thought he was saying?

"I can't bear to be without you, Holly." He caressed her hand with his thumb. "I guess what I'm asking is will you let me court you?"

Holly blew out the breath she didn't realize she was holding. "You want to court me?"

His smile collapsed. "Am I really that terrible that you would refuse?" He frowned and looked even more upset than he had earlier. "I like you, Holly. Far more than I ever thought possible."

Her heart skipped and warmth filled her. Marcus wanted to court her. She wasn't sure what she'd imagined he wanted to say to her, but a formal request to court her was not one of them.

Marcus paid the bill and helped Holly into her coat. She pulled on her gloves and they left *Ma's Kitchen*. The snow wasn't too heavy yet, so they decided to take a stroll down Dewberry Lane. He hooked his arm through Holly's and they began their exploration. Holly wanted to check out the Christmas decorations in the other stores. They stopped outside *Buttons and Bows*, and she sighed.

"Ivy's store looks marvelous," she said quietly. She hadn't owned the store very long after inheriting it from her aunt, but she'd outdone most of the other stores.

"Enthusiasm," Marcus said. "I'm sure it will wear off." And he was certain it would. He couldn't begin to imagine having to decorate your place of business every year simply because it was expected. He felt quite thankful he didn't have a storefront to maintain.

Holly turned to him and smiled. "You are always so positive. I like that about you." Despite her words, he felt there was something that she wasn't happy about. She'd agreed to let him court her, adding the whole town already believed he was. He'd tried not to laugh but couldn't quite manage it.

"What's bothering you?" He didn't meant to blurt out the words, but now they were out, there was not a thing he could do about it.

"Bothering me?"

"It feels like there's some sort of barrier between us, but I have no idea what it is." When he stared into her face, she glanced to the ground. He was right, but whether she would admit it was another thing altogether. And then it hit him. "You're still mad at me for carrying you out of the store during the fire, aren't you?"

They arrived at a wooden bench, and he guided her to sit. "I guess," she said, her eyes looking everywhere except at him.

"If it had been anyone else, would you feel the same?"

Her head shot up and she studied him closely. Holly licked her lips before answering. "Absolutely. You were a complete stranger, like the rest of the firemen."

"Forgive me?" He moved closer to her and she leaned her head against his chest. His arm came up around her, and it suddenly felt like all was right in the world.

"I forgive you," she finally said. His relief was palpable – he didn't want that hanging between them for the rest of their lives. They stayed like that for what felt like an eternity, and Marcus didn't want to ever move. But it was cold out there, and they had to move eventually. He stood and pulled her up with him. He glanced down into her face, and brought his hand up to caress her cheek. Before he could stop himself, Marcus leaned in and kissed her. This time, Holly didn't resist. Instead, she kissed him back.

Chapter Seven

It was less than a week until Christmas, and Holly was busier than ever. The last few Christmas puddings were in the pots on the stove, and her last six Christmas cakes in the oven. That would give her a couple of spares for those who forgot to order. Most of her customers planned well ahead, which helped Holly to do the same.

She had three dozen cupcakes sitting on the table waiting to be decorated. She'd added layers of green, red, and white icing to the icing bag. The result would be a Christmas tree look, with no two cupcakes looking the same. Holly loved Christmas, and everything it allowed her to be. She was not a frivolous person, and was generally quite predictable, some might even call her boring. But this time of year, her heart filled with hope, and she believed anything was possible.

The bell over the door tinkled and she went into the store. With the door open, she could hear the festive music being played outside on Dewberry Lane. The small group of three musicians smiled at her as she waved to them. The atmosphere in the small town always warmed her heart this time of year.

"Good morning, Mrs. Jensen. I have your order ready." She smiled at her long-time customer. As much as she would love to have some new customers, most of those she had were loyal customers since the store opened. In fact, some of them had urged her to open her little cake shop before it was something she'd decided to do.

"Good morning, Holly. You look pleased with yourself." She took the package Holly offered her.

"The holidays always make me happy," she said.

The woman grinned. "Not to mention that handsome young man courting you." She raised an eyebrow, no doubt expecting Holly to respond. But she didn't, so Mrs. Jensen left and Holly went back to her decorating.

She'd no sooner begun, and the bell jingled again. This time, it was Marcus. "Don't you have work to do?"

"Hello to you too," he said, eyebrows quirked. "I thought you'd be happy to see me. Besides, no one has work done this time of year unless it's an emergency." He began to pull his coat off.

"Oh, no you don't," Holly said. "I have heaps of work to do, and you're a distraction."

That made him grin. "Well, don't let me stop you. I'll fill the kettle for a coffee, shall I?" He leaned in and kissed her, and a shiver went down Holly's spine. How would she get anything done with him sitting there and watching her?

"Coffee would be nice. Oh," she said as though remembering something she'd forgotten, "would you mind checking the front door? It seems to be jamming at times. Some of the older ladies are having a world of trouble opening it."

"Sure. I'll fill the kettle then check it out."

It was good having her own handyman. The bell over the door jingled as Marcus left the kitchen. As though to prove her point, Mrs. Grayson was unable to move the door. "Let me," Marcus said, hurrying to help her. He let the older woman in then pushed and shoved the door, trying to figure out the problem. "Looks like it's buckled in the weather," Marcus said. "I can fix it this afternoon."

Holly frowned. What a nuisance but there was nothing she could do about it. "Good morning, Mrs.

Grayson. Thank you, Marcus. That would be wonderful." ·

Mrs. Grayson studied her then leaned in and spoke quietly. "What luck you have a carpenter at your beck and call." She grinned then leaned back.

Holly couldn't help but smile. She was even more convinced her best customer had set her up, but she no longer cared. With Marcus courting her, Holly's life felt complete.

With her shop door fixed, all her Christmas orders completed, and Marcus by her side, Holly was deliriously happy. Shortly, a small group of ladies were coming to watch her cake decorating demonstration – her contribution to the Dewberry Lane Christmas Extravaganza.

Every Christmas, each store undertook some sort of demonstration to entice new customers into their stores. There were often a lot of current customers, but that was good too; it built goodwill. Holly had baked an additional two dozen cupcakes and would demonstrate a simple decorating technique.

She had a variety of colored icing prepared in four icing bags. The cupcakes she would use for the demonstration were already on the table. Only another few minutes and…the door suddenly flew open and four ladies pushed their way into the store.

"Ladies, hello!" They all seemed excited to be there, and Holly was equally excited to show them her skills. "Come through to the kitchen, please."

As they made their way to her normally off-limits kitchen, they glanced about. "Oooh, Marcus did a wonderful job," Mrs. Grayson said. Holly wondered why she even came since she had her own live-in cook, but had long ago understood the woman was lonely. She spent the majority of most days here in town.

"He certainly did," Holly said proudly. "It's far better than the original." She picked up four aprons and handed one to each woman. They all looked confused "To protect your lovely gowns," she told them, then proceeded to demonstrate on one of the cupcakes. She was met with a lot of ooohs and aaahs. "Now, it's your turn." The look of surprise on their faces was priceless and filled Holly with joy.

She handed a cupcake to each woman, along with an icing bag. "I have a new level of appreciation for your expertise," Mrs. Grayson said.

"I must agree," Mrs. Carson said. "I don't know how you do it, Holly."

"Take your time and don't be intimidated. That's probably the best advice I can give you."

Mrs. Jensen raised her eyebrows. "Well, it's fun, but I won't be trying this at home." She turned to Holly and grinned. "Your job is safe, my dear. I wouldn't want to do this for a living."

Mrs. Herbert nodded. "I am totally in agreeance with you, Mrs. Jensen."

Never did Holly have illusions they would master the technique, but it was a good way to prove her worth to her customers. She handed each woman another cupcake, and swapped the icing bags about so they had a difficult color this time. "Have another try." They stared at her. "Have some fun. Don't worry how they come out."

This time around was better, but definitely not a level Holly needed to worry about.

The bell over the door jingled and Holly excused herself and hurried out to the store. Her heart fluttered when she saw Marcus standing in the middle of her shop. "I missed you," he said, as he strolled toward her. He pulled her into his arms and held her tight.

"I can't," she said. "I have a demonstration happening."

"Looks like it's finished," he whispered. When she heard the laughter in his voice, she glanced up to see the four ladies grinning at them.

~*~

Marcus rarely came to town. That is, until he met Holly.

It hadn't taken a lot of convincing on Mrs. Grayson's part to offer his services to restore the *Holly-Berry Cake Shoppe* after the fire. Especially since he hadn't forgotten the feel of Holly Yates in his arms. Those few minutes holding her had felt like a lifetime, until he'd put her down. Then he'd felt as though he wanted to do it all again.

He should have known when he saw the look on the Mrs. Grayson's face what she was up to. She had been a wonderful support to his mother all those years ago and had always kept in touch. Every birthday and at Christmas, she'd arrived with an arm full of gifts for him. Often in between times as well. She'd ensured his mother was looked after too, never allowing her birthday to go by without recognition. She was like an aunt to Marcus, although out of respect, he'd always called her Mrs. Grayson, despite her protests.

Now he'd gotten to know her, he felt rather lost since he'd finished work at Holly's shop. The distance between them only made his heart grow fonder.

"It's time," he said, ducking his head around the kitchen door. "Everyone is outside and ready."

Holly pulled her apron over her head and cleaned her hands. She'd planned on this, as everyone else on Dewberry Lane had as well. Marcus was glad she'd agreed to close the store for the short time it took to raise the Christmas tree. It was a totally new concept for Dewberry but promised to become a tradition.

When Ivy Henderson, the newcomer to town, had suggested the tree, the Christmas Extravaganza committee were thrilled. The turnout of people standing around and waiting for the raising was far more than Marcus had anticipated. He grabbed her hand as Holly finished buttoning her coat and pulled her outside.

"It's magnificent," Holly exclaimed as it was pulled into place with ropes. Marcus had spent the majority of his morning helping place those ropes, along with several other young men from Dewberry. He loved this little town and never ceased to be amazed by the level of community spirit.

"Ooooh." Holly's face lit up with excitement as the tree was pulled upright and secured. Marcus glanced about – everyone looked so happy. Several boxes had been placed near the tree for donations of toys and food for the less fortunate. Not that she would tell anyone, but Mrs. Grayson had spent a small fortune ensuring all the children in Dewberry received at least one gift on Christmas day. Marcus knew as he'd helped place them there.

The Christmas spirit was well and truly alive, and it filled his heart with joy.

Marcus put his arm around Holly. Despite the snow and the cold, warmth filled his very being. Not in his wildest dreams did he believe he would be standing here with the woman he loved. It wasn't so long ago he hadn't even met her.

"Holly." He stared into her face, then lifted his hand and brushed snow from her hair. "I need to ask you something."

She was still smiling, and it made his heart happy. She worked so hard and rarely took a break. It was especially bad this time of year, she'd told him. Holly glanced at him.

"I'm listening," she said, still somewhat distracted by what was going on around them.

"Ah, Holly, Marcus. What a lovely new tradition we have in Dewberry." Mrs. Grayson wiped the snow from her face with a gloved hand. "I do love a white Christmas," she said. "But it is rather chilly."

She was right. It was cool out here. He needed to find somewhere warmer and far more private. He turned to Holly. "Let's go back to the store. I need to talk to you."

She frowned but hurried toward the store. "It is rather cold out here, despite being rugged up." Once inside, they discarded their coats and gloves, and scurried into the kitchen where it was warmer. "I'll make us both some coffee. That will warm us up."

It sounded good, but he had a better way to get warm. He reached out and grabbed her hand, pulling Holly back to him. He enveloped her in his arms and held her close. She leaned into him, and Marcus knew they were meant to be together. He lifted her face with his fingers and kissed her. When he pulled back, he spoke quietly. "I love you, Holly. I think I have from that first day we met."

"I love you too," she said, snuggling into him. "I wasn't living before I met you. Just going through the motions."

Marcus knew exactly what she meant because he felt the same way himself. He suddenly remembered he'd brought her here for a reason and gently pushed her away. He suddenly dropped to one knee. "Holly," he said with emotionally, "will you marry me?"

Holly gasped. He'd obviously taken her unawares. Tears streamed down her face. "Yes," she said through her tears. "A million times yes!"

They'd spent a lovely Christmas Day with Mrs. Grayson, which had been a tradition for Marcus for some years. Since they were now engaged, and the talk of the town, not to mention everyone's Christmas dinner table, they'd decided on a small wedding a few days after Christmas, dependent on the preacher's availability.

Marcus stood nervously at the front of the church with the preacher. He sensed Holly at the back of the church and turned around. She looked even more beautiful than normal and was wearing the beautiful gown Mrs. Grayson had brought as a wedding gift. Marcus couldn't help but stare; in a matter of minutes, Holly would be his wife. Never in a million years would he have predicted he'd been standing here now waiting to be married.

Preacher Abraham Flannery cleared his throat then beckoned for Holly to approach as the organ music began. Mrs. Grayson leaned in and whispered something to her. Marcus could only imagine what it might be. Some womanly wisdom perhaps? His heart pounded as Holly approached. Marcus was overwhelmed by the moment.

They'd decided on a small wedding, but most of the town had turned out. Everyone knew Holly as well as Marcus, so he really shouldn't be surprised. The preacher whispered something to him, but Marcus' concentration was elsewhere.

"The ring," Preacher Flannery said. "Did you remember the ring?"

Marcus reached into his pocket and breathed a sigh of relief. It was there. He then turned his attention back to Holly, who was now standing next to him. He reached an arm around her and pulled her close. His arm dropped away after a glaring stare from the preacher.

"Dearly Beloved, we are gathered here today…"

The ceremony seemed to take forever, but Marcus knew it had only taken around fifteen minutes. His gaze never leaving her face, he slipped the gold ring on Holly's finger as he said his vows, his heart pounding. That ring represented their love and their vows to love one another to be together forever more.

"I, Marcus Jonathan Taylor, take thee, Holly Elizabeth Yates, to be my wedded wife, to have and to hold from this day forward, for better, for worse, for richer, for poorer, in sickness and in health, to love and to cherish, till death do us part, according to God's holy ordinance; and thereto I pledge thee my faith." The thought they would be together from now until forever set his heart alight. He loved her more than he ever believed possible.

After Holly said her vows, the preacher declared them husband and wife. "You may now kiss your bride."

And that's exactly what Marcus did. Until the preacher cleared his throat to remind them where they were. Holly hooked her arm through his, ready for the walk back down the aisle. Marcus had other plans, and lifted her into his arms in the same way he had on that fateful day they'd met. She stared into his eyes, and Marcus knew she was completely aware of what he was doing, only this time, she didn't protest. Which suited him perfectly. She leaned her head against his chest and wrapped her arms around his neck.

When he glanced up, dear Mrs. Grayson grinned at him wickedly. She'd been such an influence in his life, and that wasn't about to change now. He carried his wife down the aisle, only putting her to the ground once they were outside, where they were showered with rice and rose petals.

Marcus always knew God had a plan for him, but had become impatient. Now he was about to embark on that plan and couldn't be happier.

Epilogue

Nearly two years later…

Holly stared out the window as snow fell. Trees and roads were covered in snow, along with her small garden. It was white everywhere she looked, and for once she enjoyed it. Heat radiated from the roaring fire and warmth filled the room.

She glanced across at the small Christmas tree sitting in the corner of the room, the one they'd chosen together. She noticed the purring cat sleeping under the tree. Marrying Marcus was the best decision she'd ever made.

She could hear Marcus cluttering about in the kitchen and relaxed in her chair. She glanced down at the tiny bundle sound asleep in her arms.

Elizabeth Mary Taylor had a full head of midnight black hair like her father.

Holly glanced up as Marcus placed a mug of tea on the side table and took the baby out of her mother's arms. Lizzie, as they called her, did a little dance that was more like a shiver, then glanced up at her father. "Papa," she said in her baby voice, then grinned. Her little arms went out, indicating she wanted a hug. She was so much like her father it was uncanny. Warmth filled Holly watching the two of them together.

"You should lay down and have a rest yourself," Marcus said, still holding Lizzie. "I can watch her."

"Like you watched her pull down the Christmas tree?" Holly was only half joking, but it was true. The last time Marcus had offered to watch their daughter, she'd single-handedly tipped over the tree, trying to reach the decorations. All the while he snoozed on the nearby chair.

"I'll take her to the nursery and keep her safe, I promise." His mouth quirked up in a smile. She shouldn't taunt him like this, but she did like to stir him up at times.

Holly endeavored to stand, but had difficulty. Marcus was by her side almost immediately. He put Lizzie to the floor and helped his wife up.

"You look really tired," he said, glancing across at the baby crawling toward the cat. Or perhaps the tree was her target.

Holly nodded toward their baby. "Better rescue the cat before any harm is inflicted."

"She just wants to play," Marcus said, defending the baby.

"I know, but she doesn't understand. It's up to us to teach her." Holly rubbed her hands across her swollen belly, and Marcus glanced at her.

"Is everything all right?" She could see the worry on his face as he snatched Lizzie up and into his arms.

"I…I think so," she said, then winced in pain. "On second thought, perhaps not. The baby is due any day now. Maybe you should get Doc Wigham. You can leave Lizzie here."

"That," Marcus said with emphasis, "is never going to happen. You need to lay down now." He led her to the bed, and her water broke before they got there. He placed the baby in her crib while he assisted his wife, ensuring she was comfortable.

"Marcus," she called as he was leaving the room. He turned back to face her. Holly beckoned him closer and hugged him tight when he was close. "I love you," she said. "No matter what happens, I want you to remember that."

"I love you too," he said with emotion in his voice. "You will survive this. We know Matthew Wigham is an excellent doctor. One of the best." He pulled the covers up over her and began to leave again, glancing back over his shoulder as he did so.

Lizzie had been calling for her Papa to take her from the crib, but now stopped, indicating Marcus had taken her with him. Holly closed her eyes to rest them and was soon asleep, even with her labor pains.

It seemed like forever since Holly had gone into labor, and Marcus was beyond concerned. He had faith in the doctor; he'd successfully delivered Lizzie, and Holly had no aftereffects. She was so well in fact, she'd insisted on returning to the *Holly-Berry Cake Shoppe* only a month later. They'd installed an experienced pastry chef to take over because it would be impossible for Holly to work full-time with a small baby. With two babies, it would be even more difficult.

He'd brought up selling the business, but Holly would have none of it. This way, Holly said, she could still spend some time in the store when it suited her. The thing that mattered most to Marcus was his wife's happiness.

"Your mother would have been besotted with Lizzie." Mrs. Grayson spoke quietly as she glanced down at the small child in her arms. "I wish she could be here now." She stared at Marcus with sad eyes.

"Mother would have adored Lizzie." He swallowed back the emotion that threatened to overtake him. "At least they have you, their surrogate grandmother."

He watched as the older woman fought back tears. He'd only seen her cry twice before – at her husband's funeral, then at the funeral for Marcus' mother. He reached out and patted her hand. He loved that she was part of his family now. She liked to show a tough exterior, but he knew she was a softie from way back.

The door to the bedroom suddenly opened and Doc Wigham rushed out. "You can come and meet your son now," he said quietly, then hurried back in the room again.

"I have a son," he told Mrs. Grayson. "I have a son!"

"Well then, you'd better hurry up and meet him," the older lady said.

He rushed in, not certain what he'd find since there'd been no mention of Holly. The nurse held the tightly wrapped baby, but when he glanced at Holly, his heart hammered. She lay out on the bed, and didn't appear to be moving. "Is she…" He couldn't voice the words he didn't want to say. A small groan escaped her lips as Holly repositioned herself on the bed. His relief was immense.

"Your wife is exhausted," the nurse said, handing the baby to Marcus. "She needs to sleep."

He stared down into the face of his son, and tears rolled down his face. Marcus squatted down next the bed and gently kissed Holly's forehead. Her eyes fluttered open. "You rest," he said quietly, and soon she was asleep again. "I love you more than life itself," he said quietly, and meant every word.

Marcus wandered out into the sitting room with his son. They'd already decided on a name; Charles Walter Taylor if it was a boy, honoring each of their fathers.

"He's beautiful," Mrs. Grayson said after Marcus told her his name. Lizzie woke up from her nap and was excited to see her little brother.

Sitting in a comfortable chair, holding his new son, Marcus said a silent prayer of thanks to the Lord for all the riches he'd provided in the way of his family. He felt truly blessed to be part of God's plan.

The End

From the Author

Thank you so much for reading my book – I hope you enjoyed it.

I would greatly appreciate you leaving a review where you purchased, even if it is only a one-liner. It helps to have my books more visible!

About the Author

Multi-published, award-winning and bestselling author, Cheryl Wright, former secretary, debt collector, account manager, writing coach, and shopping tour hostess, loves reading.

She writes both historical and contemporary western romance, as well as romantic suspense.

She lives in Melbourne, Australia, and is married with two adult children and has six grandchildren. When she's not writing, she can be found in her craft room making greeting cards.

Links:

Website: *http://www.cheryl-wright.com/*

Blog: *http://romance-authors.com/*

Facebook Reader Group:
https://www.facebook.com/groups/cherylwrightauth or/

Join My Newsletter:

https://cheryl-wright.com/newsletter/

www.ingramcontent.com/pod-product-compliance
Lightning Source LLC
Chambersburg PA
CBHW070632120726
47909CB00004B/1398